W9-BZE-309

What's your favorite treasure?

"I have a teddy bear that used to be my mom's, and now it's mine. That's my best treasure." —Nava

"Math because it teaches you to add and subtract." —Jason

"My electric piano." —Joey

WITHDRAWN

"My school. School is very special to me because I learn a lot and have fun. That's why it's my favorite treasure." —Harrison

"My family, of course. My family is my favorite treasure." —Lia

Visit all the states with
Finn and Molly in

MAGIC ON THE MAP!

MAGIC ON THE MAP ③
TEXAS TREASURE

COURTNEY SHEINMEL & BIANCA TURETSKY

illustrated by STEVIE LEWIS

A STEPPING STONE BOOK™

Random House 🏠 New York

For William Buda & Archie Sheinmel
—C.S.
For Peter, Andreas, and Luci
—B.T.
The authors wish to thank Machaia McClenny
for her generous help with the manuscript.

This is a work of fiction. Names, characters, places, and incidents either are the product of the authors' imagination or are used fictitiously. Any resemblance to actual persons, living or dead, events, or locales is entirely coincidental.

Text copyright © 2020 by Courtney Sheinmel and Bianca Turetsky
Cover art and interior illustrations copyright © 2020 by Stevie Lewis

All rights reserved. Published in the United States by Random House Children's Books, a division of Penguin Random House LLC, New York.

Random House and the colophon are registered trademarks and A Stepping Stone Book and the colophon are trademarks of Penguin Random House LLC.

Visit us on the Web!
rhcbooks.com

Educators and librarians, for a variety of teaching tools,
visit us at RHTeachersLibrarians.com

Library of Congress Cataloging-in-Publication Data
Names: Sheinmel, Courtney, author. | Turetsky, Bianca, author. | Lewis, Stevie, illustrator.
Title: Texas treasure / Courtney Sheinmel and Bianca Turetsky; illustrated by Stevie Lewis.
Description: New York: Random House, [2020] | Series: Magic on the map; #3 | "A STEPPING STONE BOOK." | Summary: "Parker twins Finn and Molly help new friend Carlos follow a treasure map left to him by his grandfather"—Provided by publisher. Includes authors' note about the Alamo and Texas state facts.
Identifiers: LCCN 2019001905 | ISBN 978-1-9848-9569-1 (trade) | ISBN 978-1-9848-9571-4 (ebook) | ISBN 978-1-9848-9570-7 (lib. bdg.)
Subjects: | CYAC: Maps—Fiction. | Buried treasure—Fiction. | Recreational vehicles—Fiction. | Magic—Fiction. | Brothers and sisters—Fiction. | Twins—Fiction. | Alamo (San Antonio, Tex.)—Fiction. | Texas—Fiction.
Classification: LCC PZ7.S54124 Tex 2020 | DDC [Fic]—dc23

Printed in the United States of America
10 9 8 7 6 5 4 3 2 1

This book has been officially leveled by using the F&P Text Level Gradient™ Leveling System.

Random House Children's Books supports the First Amendment
and celebrates the right to read.

Contents

PROLOGUE

On the last day of second grade, twins Finn and Molly Parker came home to find a camper in their driveway. It was white with orange and yellow stripes, a rounded roof, and three windows on each side. It looked just like an ordinary camper.

That night, Molly and Finn couldn't sleep. They snuck outside to check out the camper. Finn climbed into the driver's seat and spun the wheel around. He and Molly knew that they couldn't go anywhere. They didn't have the keys. And besides, they were too young to drive!

But something weird happened . . . the camper started *talking* to them. It wasn't an ordinary camper, after all—it had a PET!

Not a pet like a cat or a dog, or even an iguana. *This* PET stood for:

Planet

Earth

Transporter.

PET explained that it used the *information superhighway* to travel anywhere in the world, in a matter of seconds. And then, faster than you could say, "Buckle up," the camper took off!

When it landed, the doors popped open.

"I'll be back when your work here is done," PET said, and it shut down.

Molly and Finn didn't know where they were or what in the world their work was. But they knew there was only one way to find out, and they headed outside.

Where will the magic camper take Finn and Molly next? You'll just have to keep reading to find out. . . .

Chapter 1

FINN'S TURN

The third night of summer vacation was a hot one. But Finn Parker didn't turn on his air-conditioner. He wanted to make sure he heard the *click* of his parents' bedroom door closing. That click would mean that they'd gone to sleep for the night and the coast was clear.

His parents were taking a long time getting to bed. Finn felt his eyelids growing heavy, and he shook himself awake.

No. No. NO! he told himself. *Don't go to sleep. You can't go to sleep.*

He would *not* go to sleep.

But Finn was really tired. He hadn't slept much since school let out. Coach Russo had made his Little League team, the Moonwalkers, run around doing ground-ball drills all day. And then there was the camper.

The *magic* camper, with a talking PET (aka Planet Earth Transporter) that could travel anywhere in the world in a matter of seconds! Just two days ago, Dad had traded with one of the other professors at the college where he worked—his car for Professor Vega's camper. Dad didn't know the camper was magic. It was possible that even Professor Vega didn't know.

Finn and his twin sister, Molly, had

discovered the magic that first night. They snuck into the camper after bedtime. PET turned on and whisked them off to Colorado, where they rescued a cow named Snowflake. The next night, they went to New York, where they met the star of Molly's favorite TV show, Hallie Hampton, who sent them on a scavenger hunt all around the city.

Finn knew exactly where he wanted to go this time . . . as soon as his parents' door clicked shut.

He decided he'd rest while he waited for the click. He closed his eyes and waited. And waited. And . . .

There was a knock on his door. Finn's eyelids flicked open. Molly was standing in the doorway. "Finn?" she whispered.

"Yeah?"

"Did you fall asleep?" Molly asked.

Finn sat up quickly. "What? No. Of course not!"

"*Shh,*" Molly said. Her eyes flashed toward their parents' bedroom door. "You'll wake them up."

"I didn't fall asleep," Finn whispered.

"Because if you're too tired—"

"I'm wide awake," Finn said. He swung his legs out of bed. He was in his pajamas, but he didn't need to change into regular clothes. As long as he had his trusty Moonwalkers hat on, he was good to go.

He and Molly crept down the stairs and out of the house, closing the front door softly behind them. They walked down the drive-way and stepped up into the main room of the camper, which was a kitchen, a dining room, and a bedroom, all rolled into one. The counter turned into a table, the couch turned into a bed, and the cabinet turned into a TV.

Molly walked to the very back. A map of the world was pinned onto a bulletin board. So far, she and Finn had put three pushpins in the map: one in Colorado, one in New York, and one in their home state of Ohio, where they'd lived all their lives.

Molly touched each pushpin. The tips of her fingers felt little sparks. "I wonder where the next one will go," she said.

"I know exactly where it's going," Finn said. "Since you picked where we went last night, I'm picking tonight."

"Where?" Molly asked.

"I can give you a hint," Finn said. "The

Reds are playing there this weekend!"

"The Reds . . . the Reds . . . ," Molly said. "Is that something about baseball?"

"Duh," Finn said. "They're a team: the Cincinnati Reds."

"You want to go to Cincinnati? Right here in Ohio?"

"No. I want to go where they're playing their next game," Finn said.

"And where is that?"

"As PET would say, that's for me to know and you to find out. Come on!"

Finn ran toward the big leather seats in the front of the camper. "I'm coming," Molly said from right behind him.

"Remember—I get the driver's seat," Finn said.

"I know, I know."

Molly sat in the passenger seat. The twins buckled their seat belts. Finn put his hands on the wheel and looked at the screen on the dashboard. "C'mon, PET," he said. "Wake up! I'm ready to pick my destination!"

But the screen remained dark.

"Make sure you're *thinking* of your destination," Molly said. "I was thinking of mine when PET turned on the last time."

"I'm thinking of it," Finn said. He pushed the POWER button next to PET's screen a bunch of times. Nothing happened. Seconds ticked by and turned into minutes.

"I guess maybe . . . maybe the magic ran out," Molly said. "It's too bad. I made a new friendship bracelet to give away."

Finn took off his Moonwalkers cap and shook his head. "It's not fair," he said. "PET picked the first destination, and you picked the second one. I never got a turn."

Molly undid her seat belt and stood up. "If we're not going anywhere, we should go back to bed," she said.

Finn put his cap back on. He undid his seat belt. But just as he started to stand up from his seat, the screen lit up. The word "WELCOME" appeared in all red letters.

"PET!" Finn cried. "Look, Molly! There's magic left, after all!"

"Sorry, kids," PET's robotic voice said. "My server needed to warm up."

"Yay, you're back!" Molly said.

"Back and ready to go," PET said. "Finn has chosen our next destination."

"Holy guacamole!" Finn cried. "It really worked!"

"You two better buckle up."

The twins pulled at their seat belts and clicked them into place, just in time. The camper started to hum, and then it shook. There was a flash of white light, and they were off!

Chapter 2

BACK IN TIME?

Molly pressed her nose to the window. "I see mockingbirds!" she cried.

"Where?" Finn asked.

"Over there—see their gray and white feathers?"

"Oh yeah," he said.

The camper flew over thin green trees, stretches of sand dunes, and a canyon with red rocks.

"Is that the Grand Canyon?" Finn asked.

"No, I don't think so. This doesn't look as long or as deep," Molly replied.

"It looks pretty long and deep to me," Finn said. "But I don't see what I'm really looking for."

"I can't help if I don't know what it is," Molly said.

"Minute Maid Park," Finn said. "The stadium where the Houston Astros play."

"Houston?" Molly said. "The city in Texas?"

"Yep."

"Wow—the Lone Star State," Molly said. "Home of the Rio Grande and the NASA space center!"

"And the Houston Astros, who are hosting the Cincinnati Reds *tonight*," Finn said.

"The Astros are a good team. Maybe the Reds need my help—like, they could need me to catch a fly ball, or even fill in for one of the guys."

"I don't think they'd let a kid fill in for a major-league baseball player," Molly said. "No matter how good you are."

"We won't know until we get there," Finn said. The camper landed with a thud. "Whoa! We're here already? At Minute Maid Park?"

PET didn't answer. Instead it said what it always said when the twins arrived at a new destination: "I'll be back when your work here is done."

And with that, the screen went dark. The camper doors popped open. Molly and Finn undid their seat belts and stepped outside into a grassy courtyard.

"Whew, it's hot," Molly said. "Even hotter than Ohio. Good thing I'm in this sundress. I love the cowboy boots, too."

"Oh no. Oh no. Oh no," Finn said. "Do *not* tell me I'm wearing an Astros jersey! I can't do that to the Reds!"

He looked down to see what he was wearing: a plaid button-down shirt, jeans, and a wide belt with a big silver buckle.

"Oh, phew," he said. "Our only problem is finding the stadium. Let's ask someone . . . maybe that guy."

He pointed to a man in a brown jacket and a matching wide-brimmed hat.

"Why would someone be wearing a jacket in this weather?" Molly asked.

Finn shrugged. "It doesn't matter. We're asking him for directions, not fashion advice."

Before Finn could step forward to talk to him, the man threw up his arms and shouted, "What are we going to do? General Santa Anna and his men are coming!"

"Santa Anna . . . Santa Anna," Molly said. "That name is kind of familiar."

"Not to me," Finn said. "But from the sound of it, I doubt it's anyone I'd want to meet."

Another man strode across the courtyard. He was carrying a crate under his arm and wearing a fur hat with a striped tail hanging off the back. Maybe he was Santa Anna! Finn and Molly scooted back and hid behind a wall, just in case.

Other people came forward and gathered around the man in a semicircle.

"Is that who I think it is?" a woman asked loudly.

"I think so," a man answered.

"I heard he killed a hundred bears in one season," the woman said.

"I heard he can ride a streak of lightning," the man replied.

"Oh my goodness," Molly whispered to Finn. "That man with the crate—I think he's Davy Crockett!"

"Now, that name *is* familiar," Finn said. "Does he work with Dad at the college?"

"Of course not," Molly said. "We learned about Davy Crockett in Ms. Gitty's class. Back in the olden days, he was a soldier and a politician. He died in the Battle of the Alamo."

"If he died, then he's definitely not the guy standing in front of us, because that guy is *alive*."

"I know. But look at what he's standing in front of. It looks like an old church, right?"

"Yeah. So?"

"So that's just what the Alamo looked like in our social studies textbook," Molly said. "The battle that happened there was the most important battle in the whole Texas Revolution. It happened almost *two hundred years ago,* in 1836. That must be why everyone's wearing funny clothes. They're olden-day clothes."

"Are you saying they're all ghosts?" Finn asked, his voice quivering.

"No, of course not," Molly said.

"Phew."

"I'm saying we've gone back in time."

"That's not possible," Finn whispered, his

face suddenly pale. "PET told us it wasn't a time machine."

"PET is magic. *Anything* is possible."

The man put down the crate he was holding and climbed up onto it. "I'm Davy Crockett!" he cried.

"Holy guacamole," Finn said softly.

"You may know me as the King of the Wild Frontier," Crockett said. "General Santa Anna and his men are on their way here right now. They want us to surrender so that Texas remains a part of Mexico. But I will help you fight for an independent Texas!"

There were cheers from the crowd.

"And afterward," he continued, "we'll have a fandango to celebrate, and I'll play my fiddle. There's a lot of work to do before that, though. Who's with me?"

Molly's and Finn's eyes met. They knew they were thinking the exact same thing. And when they spoke, they said the exact same thing: "We are!"

Chapter 3

CUT!

The twins rushed over to Davy Crockett.

"CUT!" someone shouted. A man in a T-shirt and shorts strode toward the kids. "What do you two think you're doing?"

"Um . . . this is going to be hard to explain," Finn said. "We're from the future, so we know what's going to happen in this battle and, well . . ." He lowered his voice. "Mr. Crockett is going to die."

"Now, listen here—"

"It will be okay," Molly cut in. "Really. My brother and I are here to help."

"It's our work," Finn added.

"I know you don't believe us, but look at our clothes," Molly said. "This is what regular, modern-day clothes look like."

For a moment, everyone was quiet. Then the man started laughing. Around him, the others laughed, too.

"You kids," the man said between chuckles. "You really believe you stepped into the past, don't you?"

"Well, we . . . ," Finn started. He lowered his eyes and whispered to Molly, "You know, this guy is wearing regular, modern-day clothes, like we are."

"That's right, I am," the man said. "I'm a

24

director, and these people are all actors. Our play opens next week, and you just interrupted our morning dress rehearsal."

"Sorry," Molly said. "We made a mistake."

"I'll say," the man said.

"Give the kids a break, Hank," Davy Crockett said—or rather, the actor *playing* Davy Crockett said. He stuck out a hand. "My name's Andy."

"I'm Molly," Molly said.

"And I'm Finn," Finn said.

"We're really embarrassed," Molly said, and Finn nodded. Their cheeks were pink.

"Ah, don't be embarrassed," Andy said. "I think it's mighty brave that y'all were willing to help. Fortunately, Texas already won its independence from Mexico and became part of the United States. That's what our play is all about."

"Let's wrap rehearsal for today," Hank said. "Meet back here tomorrow morning, okay?"

"Sure thing," Andy said. He pulled off his fur cap. "Gosh, it feels good to get this off my head. It's too hot for a coonskin cap."

"Coonskin . . . as in *raccoon*?" Finn asked.

"Well, not a real one. This thing is just acting the part, same as me."

"That's good," Molly said. "I wouldn't

want a raccoon to get hurt for a hat. Can I ask you something?"

"Sure," Andy said.

"I love new words, and you used a word that I'd never heard: 'fandango.' What does that mean?"

"It's a kind of party they used to have here at the Alamo, where they'd dance the night away," Andy explained.

"Cool. Thank you."

"Oh, I have a question, too," Finn said. "As long as we're here in modern times, do you know how to get to Minute Maid Park?"

"Minute Maid Park?" Andy asked. "You mean in Houston where the Astros play?"

"Yep."

"Well, that's a good two hundred miles from here in San Antonio. Tell your parents they've gotta drive down Interstate 45 to Interstate 10, and then—"

"Never mind," Finn said.

Molly put a hand on Finn's shoulder. "Texas is the second biggest state in the United States," she said. "I guess next time you pick the destination, you need to be more specific about it."

"Oh man," Finn said. He shook his head. "And we didn't even get to save Davy Crockett."

"It was probably pretty silly to think we could have," Molly admitted. "We don't know anything about fighting a battle."

"That's true," Finn said. He looked up at Davy Crockett . . . err, Andy. "Thanks for your help," he said. "But now we gotta go. We have work to do!"

Chapter 4

FOLLOW THAT KID

"I knew we couldn't be in olden times," Finn said. "Look at all the office buildings and shops around here."

"Oh, you knew, did you?" Molly said. "Is that why you offered to save Davy Crockett with me?"

Finn's cheeks grew red. "Yeah, well . . . ," he said. "So . . . do you think our work is in the Alamo?"

Molly looked up at the old church. "There's only one way to find out," she said, and she pulled open the heavy front door.

The front room was lit by big chandeliers, and the walls were lined with state flags. "Look," Finn said, pointing to a flag with a blue triangle and red and white stripes. "That's the Ohio state flag!"

"That's right," a woman in a red polo shirt said. "Hi, I'm Maria, and welcome to the Alamo! Are you two in the play?"

"We were sort of accidentally in it," Molly said.

"Well, that counts, as far as I'm concerned," Maria said. "I have free passes for you to see the museum. And here's a map so you don't miss anything."

"This building doesn't seem big enough to need a map," Finn said.

"There's a lot more to see than just what's in here," Maria said. "For example, there's the Cavalry Courtyard, the Fortress Alamo exhibit, and even more."

"Cool," Molly said. She unfolded the map and turned to her brother. "Hmm . . . could our work be by the wall of history, or the garden, or the temporary sacristy—whatever that is . . ."

"A sacristy is a place where priests prepare for a service," Maria explained.

"Another new word," Molly said. "Thanks!"

"Some people refer to that room as the monk's burial chamber instead," Maria said. "Even though it doesn't have anything to do with monks or burial. Funny thing, don't you think?"

"Yep," Molly said. She turned to Finn. "I think we should start there because it's closest."

Finn gulped and followed his sister to a small dark room without any windows. "Well, there doesn't seem to be much work to do here," he said. "Let's keep moving."

"Are you scared?" Molly asked.

"No," Finn said.

"Really? You sound scared."

"Well, okay, I am. I don't want to see ghosts again."

"We didn't see ghosts before," Molly said. "They were just actors. And we won't see ghosts now. First of all, Maria said no one is buried in here—"

"Then why do some people call it a burial chamber?" Finn asked.

"I don't know," Molly said. "But second of all, there's no such thing as ghosts."

"I hope you're right," Finn said, and shivered. "But just in case, I'm going to wait over here in the doorway." He backed up and ran right into someone. Was it the ghost of one of the buried monks?

"AHH!" he gasped.

"Sorry, I didn't mean to scare you," a kid said. He didn't look like a ghost, or like a monk. He was just an ordinary boy, about the same age as the twins. "I was just . . . I was . . ."

"Are you lost?" Molly asked.

"Oh, yeah," the boy said, nodding quickly. "That's right. I'm lost."

"I figured," Molly said. "Since you're holding a map."

"How'd you know it was a map?" the boy asked.

"We got one, too," Molly said.

"The lady in the front was handing them out," Finn added.

"Oh, right."

"Where are you trying to go?" Molly said. "We can show you, if you want."

"Ah, it's too much work, don't worry," the boy said. He stuffed his map into his back pocket.

Molly and Finn looked at each other. The boy had said the magic word: "work."

"There's no such thing as too much work," Molly said. "Right, Finn?"

"That's right," he said. "Work is our specialty. Especially if it means we can get out of this room. I'm Finn, by the way. And this is my twin sister, Molly."

"I'm Carlos," the boy said. He brushed his dark bangs from his eyes.

"We're visiting from Ohio," Finn said. "What about you?"

"I'm from right here," Carlos said. "San Antonio, Texas."

"You live here and you've *never* been to the Alamo?" Molly asked.

"Uh . . . yeah," Carlos said. "Anyway, I'm in a rush to get home."

"I know how to get us out of here," Finn said, happy to have an excuse to leave. "Right this way."

Finn and Molly led Carlos to the entrance. Carlos thanked them quickly and started to run off.

"Hang on, I have something for you," Molly said. She fiddled with the bracelet on her wrist. "After I meet a new person and help them, I like to give them a friendship bracelet," she explained. "But I did the knot too tight."

"It's okay," Carlos said. "I gotta go." He

headed off before Molly could undo the bracelet.

"That was our easiest work so far!" Finn said.

"Maybe we're just getting better at it," Molly said. "Oh, now the knot is loose enough. I guess I'll give this bracelet to the next person we help."

"Since we have extra time, maybe we can ask PET to swing by Minute Maid Park," Finn said. "You can give your bracelet to one of the players."

Molly sighed. "Okay, sure."

She and Finn waited out front, expecting to hear PET's honk to signal that it was time to head home. But all they heard were the sounds of people chatting, cars driving down nearby streets, and birds in the trees above.

"Huh," Finn said. "Do you think it's possible that PET got stuck in traffic?"

"PET doesn't take regular roads," Molly said. She glanced around. "Oh, hey, there's Carlos."

Finn looked where Molly was pointing. Carlos checked over his shoulder and walked into the Alamo's side entrance.

"I thought he wanted to go home," Finn said.

"I guess our work wasn't so easy, after all," said Molly. "Follow that kid!"

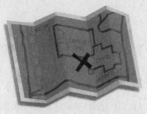

Chapter 5

X MARKS THE SPOT

"Back so soon?" Maria asked.

"Oh, yeah," Finn said. "You can never get enough history, that's my motto. Gotta go. Lots to see."

The twins moved quickly through the main hall, looking for Carlos. "This way," Molly said, heading back into the burial chamber.

But it was empty.

"It's like he just disappeared," Finn said.

"That's not possible," Molly said. "He's a kid, not a magician."

"He could be a kid who's also a magician," Finn said. "Or a—"

"Don't say it, Finn."

"You don't know what I was going to say."

"Yes, I do. You were going to say 'ghost.' But they don't exist."

A dark-haired boy hurried past the room.

"You see," Molly said. "There he is. Carlos, wait!"

But Carlos didn't stop.

"Either he didn't hear me, or he's ignoring us," Molly said.

"Or he's a ghost," Finn said.

"He's *not* a ghost!"

Molly and Finn jogged to catch up. "Hey, Carlos!" they called.

"Oh. Hi, Finn. Hi, Molly," Carlos said. He stuffed his map into his back pocket again.

"Is everything okay?" Molly asked.

"Uh-huh," Carlos said. "Why do you ask?"

"Because you said you had to rush home, but now here you are again," Molly said. "And you're hiding your map."

"What map?" Carlos asked.

"The one that just fell out of your pocket and onto the floor," Finn said.

Carlos spun around and grabbed it.

"Don't worry," Finn said. "We have our own map. We don't need yours."

"That's right," Molly said. "We want to help you. That's why we're here—at least, I think it is."

"You think you came to the Alamo to help *me*?" Carlos asked.

The twins nodded.

"Well, it's nice that you came all this way," Carlos said, "but you didn't have to. I'm not looking for anyone's help. I've gotta be brave and do what I'm doing all by myself."

Finn turned to Molly. "Maybe we're supposed to help someone else."

"Maybe," she said. "But, Carlos, you don't always have to do things by yourself. Sometimes the bravest thing is to ask for help."

"Oh my goodness," Carlos said. "You knew my grandpa!"

"Huh?" Molly asked.

"Berto Martin," Carlos said. "He told you that—about asking for help?"

"No, my teacher Ms. Gitty did," Molly said.

"Oh," Carlos said. He hung his head. "My grandpa used to say that, too. I thought maybe he sent you here, like magic."

"Since you mentioned magic . . . ," Finn said.

Molly's eyes flashed toward her brother. "*Shh,*" she said. She didn't think they should say anything about the camper. "You know what I think," she told Carlos. "I think that even if your grandpa *didn't* send us, we can still help you."

"Well . . . ," Carlos said. "What I'm doing is a secret, but okay. You can help me. Come over here."

The twins followed Carlos to a low stone bench in the corner. He carefully laid out his map on the gray marble.

"Whoa, Molly," Finn said. "That doesn't look like the map you got. It looks much older."

The uneven edges of Carlos's map were yellowed. The lines were faded and had worn off completely in some spots. There was a faint red X in the center of the paper.

"This was my grandpa's map," Carlos said softly. "He was searching for buried treasure here in the Alamo for his whole life, but he never found it."

"Buried treasure?" Finn asked. He liked the sound of that!

"Yeah," Carlos said. "And it could be worth *millions.*"

"Where did your grandpa get the map?" Molly asked.

"My great-great-great-great-great-grandfather died in the Texas Revolution. I reckon he must have buried the treasure so my family could find it. I'm not sure exactly what it is—but it's probably gold or jewels."

Finn's eyes grew wide—millions of dollars in gold and jewels. "Holy guacamole," he said.

"My grandpa died last month," Carlos said. His eyes got shiny, and he blinked a bunch. "He never found the treasure."

"Oh, I'm so sorry," Molly said.

"Me too," Finn said.

"He left this map in an envelope with my name on it," Carlos said. "I guess that means it's up to me to find it. I *need* to find it—for my grandpa—because it'd make him so proud of me. And my grandma Rosa has been so sad. She wants me to sit with her and talk about Grandpa Berto. Talking about him doesn't help anything. But finding gold and jewels . . . well, that would help a lot."

Molly and Finn nodded.

Carlos pointed to the red X on the map. "This has to be where the treasure is buried. X marks the spot, right?"

"Yeah, I guess so," Finn said. He turned to his sister. "Just like one of the clues in the New York City scavenger hunt. But I wish this X wasn't in a room that some people call a burial chamber. You know, because of the . . ."

"What?" Carlos asked.

"The ghosts," Finn said.

Molly rolled her eyes.

"I've been over it and over it," Carlos said. "And there isn't any treasure there. At least not that I can find."

"Hmm . . . ," Molly said.

"Are you thinking the ghosts stole the treasure?" Finn asked.

"No, ghosts don't exist," she said. "I'm thinking that X *usually* marks the spot. Unless . . ."

"Unless what?" Carlos asked.

"Unless X means something else."

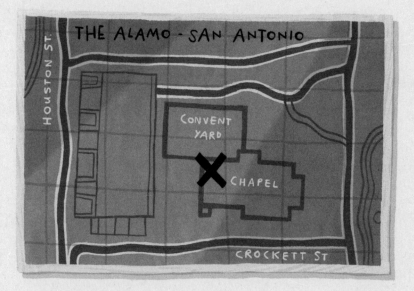

Chapter 6

LETTERS AND NUMBERS

"What else could X possibly mean?" Carlos asked.

"Oh, lots of things," Molly said.

"Are you saying there isn't any buried treasure?" Finn asked.

"Of course there is!" Carlos said. "Grandpa always said there's hidden treasure in every problem, and it's your job to find it."

Molly scrunched up her face, which she

often did when she was concentrating. "X might not really mark the spot where it's buried. It could be the first letter of someone's name, or it could stand for a number."

"Oh, I get it," Finn said. "Like if A is one and B is two, then X would be ..."

Carlos quickly recited the alphabet and counted on his fingers. "X is the twenty-fourth letter of the alphabet!" he said.

"So we're looking for the number twenty-four in here somewhere?" Finn asked.

"No, I don't think so," Molly said. "I think X means ten."

"But J is the tenth letter of the alphabet," Carlos said.

"We're looking for a J now?" Finn asked. "I don't understand."

"I'm talking about Roman numerals," Molly

said. "I read about them in the fourth-grade math textbook."

"Hang on," Carlos said. "You guys are in fourth grade? No offense, but you look way too short for that."

"No, we just finished second grade," Finn said. He turned to his sister. "What were you doing reading a fourth-grade textbook?"

Molly shrugged. "I was bored one day, so I read it," she said. "And I learned that Roman numerals are a math system that was made up in ancient Rome. You make numbers out of combinations of letters. For example, if you want to write the number one, you write a capital I. And if you want to write two, it's II."

"And let me guess," Finn said, "three would be III."

"Yep!"

"So wouldn't ten be IIIIIIIII?" Carlos asked.

"No, some numbers have their own letters," Molly explained. "Like five is V, and ten is X."

Finn shook his head. "Leave it to you to give us a lesson on ancient Roman numbers while we're visiting Texas."

"It's cool to know some fourth-grade math," Carlos said. "But I don't understand how that helps with the map."

"I think we need to go back into that room and count things in tens," Molly said. "Maybe the treasure is out the tenth window."

"But it's super dark and creepy in there, and it doesn't have any windows," Finn reminded her. "So I guess we don't have to go."

"No, we still have to go," she said. "It could be the tenth stone on the ground."

"C'mon," Carlos said, folding up the map.

He and Molly headed back down the hall. Finn followed behind. Inside the room, Carlos counted to the tenth stone on the ground, then bent down and tried to lift it up. It wouldn't budge.

"Okay, it's not ten stones," Molly said. "Try taking ten steps from the doorway and checking that spot."

Carlos took ten steps. But the stone he was standing on wouldn't budge, either.

"What if X means the tenth ghost in here?" Finn said.

"It doesn't mean that," Molly said.

"Maybe it's behind the tenth artifact on the wall," Carlos said. He reached for a framed black-and-white photograph.

"Hey there!" a guard called. "Hands off museum property!"

Carlos jumped back quickly. "Sorry," he said.

"You and your friends should run along now," the guard said.

"Oh, please can we stay for a few more minutes?" Molly asked. "We're working on a project . . . ah . . . a project for school."

"Isn't school out for the summer?" the guard asked.

"Summer school," Molly explained. "We have a history project about the Texas Revolution due next week. Do you know anything about the subject?"

The guard chuckled. "It just so happens I know nearly everything about the subject," he said.

"Oh!" Molly said. "Cool. I have so many questions. First of all, when was the Alamo built?"

"The first stone was laid in 1744," the guard said. "If you come this way, I can show you where it is. . . ."

The guard walked toward the hall. Molly looked over her shoulder and mouthed "Keep looking" to Finn and Carlos. Then she scurried along after the guard.

"Wow, Molly figured out that X could mean ten, and now she got the guard off our backs," Carlos said. "Your sister is smart as a whip!"

"You don't have to tell her that," Finn said. "She already knows. Now, let's check behind that tenth artifact."

Carlos quickly lifted the picture. "Nothing here," he reported, and he put it back.

"Hmm," Finn said. "Well, maybe it's the tenth stone on the wall instead of the floor."

Carlos counted the stones along the wall.

They were all different shapes, and the tenth one looked like the state of Texas!

"It feels loose!" Carlos said.

"Can you get it out?"

"I think so." Carlos stuck his fingers around the edges and pried the stone out of the wall. Behind it was a scroll, tied up with a piece of old twine.

"Ooh!" Finn cried. "Maybe this is why they call it the burial chamber—because something's buried in here after all!"

 Carlos grabbed the scroll and wedged the stone back into the wall. He undid the twine, and together, he and Finn unrolled the scroll.

Carlos sucked in his breath. "Oh, wow, Grandpa!" he said.

Chapter 7

THE PORTAL

"Is that another map?" Finn asked.

"Yeah, it's . . . whoa!"

"What?"

"I reckon this is the other half of the one my grandpa left me," Carlos said. He put the two together. "I thought the first map was all there is, but look at this. They fit together, and this second part says we have to go to the arcade."

"The arcade?" Finn asked. "There's an *arcade* in here?"

"That's what the map says."

"Great. Let's go there."

Finn and Carlos ran out of the dark room. Molly was down the hallway, deep in a history lesson with the museum guard.

"We found it!" Finn said. "You know, the stuff we needed for ... our report."

"Perfect!" Molly said. "Thank you so much, Mr. Collins. You've been extremely helpful. It's lucky we met you!"

"My pleasure," the guard said.

"Come on, Molly," said Finn. "Our next stop is the arcade."

Finn, Molly, and Carlos hurried down the hallway. They were one step closer to finding the treasure!

"You're in luck," Finn told Carlos. "There are two things I'm an expert at: baseball and video games. I thought I was coming to Texas to play baseball. But if we're headed to an arcade, I guess it's video games." He rubbed his hands together. "I can't wait!"

"It's so weird," Molly said.

"What are you talking about?" Finn said. "You know I'm a video game expert. You see me play my baseball video game all the time. I just got to level five!"

"I mean it's weird that there's a video arcade in the Alamo," Molly said. "What's an arcade doing at the site of a famous battle?"

"Maybe it's a video game about the battle," Finn said. "I wonder how many levels I'll have to beat to get to the treasure."

"We're almost there," Carlos said. "Just one more turn."

The kids turned the corner.

Finn looked down a narrow corridor with arches overhead. "What in the world?" he said.

"I don't see any games," Carlos said.

"There aren't any," Molly said. "I knew it didn't make sense to have an arcade in the Alamo. After all, the Alamo was built way before video games were invented. Your great-great-great-great-great-grandfather would never have heard of them!"

"I don't understand," Finn said. "Why would they call it an arcade when there aren't any games?"

"Excellent question!" a man said. He was wearing a red Alamo polo shirt, just like

Maria's. He clapped his hands. "Everyone, gather around."

A group of people circled the man. There were a few kids and even more grown-ups.

"In case you didn't hear the question, I'll repeat it for our tour group," the man said. "This young man wants to know why this space is called an arcade. I assume it's because he's used to the word 'arcade' referring to a video arcade, am I right?"

"Yeah, that's right," Finn said.

"Well, the word 'arcade' can refer to a video arcade, but it can also mean a covered passageway with arches."

"Oh, cool," Molly said. "That's my third new word today!"

"It's not a new word," Finn said. "You already knew about the video kind of arcade."

"Yeah, but now I know a whole new meaning," she said. "Besides, I knew there couldn't be an arcade at the Alamo from back in the olden days."

"Yeah, whatever," Finn grumbled.

"I hate to say I told you so . . . ," Molly said.

"That's not true," Finn said. "You love to say that."

"Any more questions?" the man asked. No one had any, so he went on: "The arcade at the Alamo was constructed in the 1930s. It's a portal to the garden."

"What's a portal?" a kid asked.

"It's an entrance," Molly whispered to Finn.

"I knew that," Finn whispered back.

"It's a doorway, a gate, or some other kind of entrance," the man told the group. "Feel free to take pictures."

People lifted their phones and cameras.

"When you're done, follow me this way to the garden, and we'll continue our tour," he said.

After everyone finished snapping pictures, the group moved on. "The coast is clear," Molly said. "Let's check for loose stones." She, Finn, and Carlos felt around the ground and over each archway, but the stones were all stuck tight.

"Now what?" Carlos asked.

"I don't know," Molly admitted. She sat down on a little stone bench to think about what to do next.

Behind the bench, there was a big tree with a thick trunk and branches that twisted around in every direction. Finn grabbed one of the branches and swung upward.

"Hey!" Molly said. "Don't do that!"

"Why not?" Finn asked.

"Because I bet you're not allowed."

"But it's a perfect climbing tree," Finn said. "Besides, if I can't play an arcade game, I might as well climb a tree." He swung up one more branch with the ease of a monkey. Then he felt the tree *move*.

"Do you hear that?" Carlos asked.

"What?" Molly asked.

As soon as the word was out of her mouth, she heard a low rumbling sound.

"Finn! Get off the tree!" Molly shouted.

Finn leapt from his perch on a high branch to a lower branch, and then to the ground. He, Molly, and Carlos backed away from the tree. They watched the tree, their eyes growing wider and wider.

A crack ran up the length of the trunk. The rumbling got louder and louder, like the sound of an airplane flying closer. The crack in the trunk broke open.

"I can't believe it," Carlos said. "Is this real? Are you seeing what I'm seeing?"

Finn's mouth was hanging open, but he nodded. The trunk had magically formed a doorway that revealed a staircase leading underground.

"I'm seeing it," Molly said. Her voice was barely a whisper. "But I can hardly believe it. Finn, you found a portal to . . . to . . . to I don't know where. But I don't think it's a garden."

"Let's see where it goes," Carlos said.

He stepped toward the doorway, and the twins followed.

Chapter 8

THE SECRET PASSAGEWAY

The kids crept down a creaky old stairwell, going lower and lower underground, and farther and farther from the sunlight above.

"This is even darker and creepier than the burial chamber," Finn said.

"That's why it's a good place to bury treasure," Molly said. "If only there was some light down here to see it better."

"Oh, I forgot I brought this," Carlos said.

He pulled something out of his pocket. There was a click, and then the staircase was illuminated by the bright beam of a flashlight.

The wooden steps were uneven and covered in dust. It looked as if no one had been down these stairs in a very long time.

"I don't know if being able to see things is making me feel better or worse," Finn said.

The rumbling sounded again. "Carlos, shine your flashlight up there," Molly said.

He pointed the light up the stairwell they'd just walked down. The kids gasped. The doorway in the tree had closed back up!

"Now what do we do?" Finn cried.

"We keep going forward," Molly said.

Carlos pointed the flashlight in front of them again. "To the treasure," he said.

"To the treasure," Molly repeated.

Finn gulped. "To the treasure," he managed to say.

"You know, I've been thinking," Carlos said. "It's not fair for me to keep everything we find all for myself. I'll give you a gold bar as payment for your help."

"Oh, you don't have to pay us anything," Molly said.

"I insist," Carlos said. "My grandpa always said the more we have, the more we should share."

"He sounds like a really generous guy," Molly said.

"He was. He'd want you to have some gold so you could buy something special."

"I'm too scared to think about that right now," Finn said.

But as they made their way down the stairs

to the mouth of a long, twisty hallway, Finn *did* think about what the gold could buy, and it made him a little bit less scared. If he ever got out of here, he'd buy season tickets to the Reds.

Scratch that. He'd buy the Great American Ball Park, where the Reds played, so he could go to every game and bring all his friends.

"It's as quiet as a tomb down here," Molly said.

"That's not funny," Finn said.

"I wasn't trying to be funny," Molly said.

"At least we have this flashlight," Carlos said.

The second he said the word "flashlight," the light went out, and all three kids screamed.

"I guess I should have checked the batteries," Carlos said.

"Oh no!" Finn cried. "I can't see my hand, and it's right in front of my face! We need to go back!"

"We can't go back," Molly said. "The tree closed up."

"So there's no way out?" Finn asked. "What's the use of finding treasure if we're stuck underground? It's not like we can buy anything down here."

"Maybe there's a door at the end of the hall," Carlos said. "Let's keep going. We can feel along the walls." He took a small step forward, and there was a tiny spark of light under his foot.

"Your shoes!" Molly said. "They're the light-up kind!"

"Oh, I forgot that, too," Carlos said. "We can use them as a backup flashlight."

"Phew," Finn said.

Carlos and his light-up sneakers led the way. But sneaker lights aren't as bright as flashlights, and the passageway was still nearly dark. Molly walked with her arms out in front of her, like a mummy, and banged into a stone wall.

"Ow!"

"You okay?" Finn asked. He rushed toward the sound of her voice, tripped over something, and fell to the ground.

"Are *you* okay?" Molly asked him.

"Yeah, I think so," Finn said. He put a hand to the ground to push himself back up. "AH! I think I tripped over . . . I can't even say it."

"What?" Molly cried.

"It feels like bones! There's a skeleton! Probably from someone who died in the Texas Revolution!"

Carlos stomped and lit up the ground with his shoes to reveal a pile of sticks.

"It's okay," Carlos said. "We've come so far, and I reckon we're almost there."

The end of the passageway was a dead end. There was no way to go forward, and with the tree entrance closed up, they couldn't go back, either.

Finn took off his Moonwalkers cap and leaned against the stone wall. Maybe the pile of sticks had turned out to *not* be a skeleton, but it was possible he, Molly, and Carlos would be skeletons down here one day.

He shivered, then looked up. "Umm . . .

hey," he said. "It looks like the only place left to go is up."

Molly and Carlos turned their eyes toward the ceiling. A thin beam of sunlight was peeking through a trapdoor above.

Finn stretched his hands up toward the door. Not even close. He jumped, but he couldn't reach it that way, either.

"What if I make a slingshot with my hands? Then you can put your foot here and I can boost you up," Carlos suggested.

"I guess I could try," Finn said.

"Pretend that you're going for a fly ball," Molly said.

Carlos weaved his fingers together. Finn put his sneaker in Carlos's hands.

"One, two, three!" the kids counted.

Carlos launched Finn toward the ceiling.

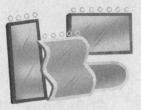

Chapter 9

THE AMAZING MIRROR MAZE

Finn managed to dislodge the trapdoor and pull himself through the hole. Carlos and Molly were left standing alone in the dark.

"Finn!" Molly called up toward where her brother had disappeared.

Finn didn't answer.

"Where do you think he is?" Carlos asked.

"I don't know," Molly said. She felt her

body tighten in fear. What if Finn had ended up in an Alamo dungeon?

But then a rope dropped down from the hole. "Grab on and climb up," Finn said. "It's so weird up here. But I promise you, I'm the real Finn."

"The real Finn?" Molly asked. "What are you talking about?"

"You'll see when you get here. Climb up."

Molly looked over at Carlos. With the little bit of light coming in from the hole in the ceiling, she could see his face. "Do you want to go first?" she asked.

"After you," Carlos said.

"Okay." She put her hand on the rope, but then she let go.

"Come on," Finn called. "Don't you want to get out of that creepy passageway?"

"Yeah, I do, but . . . ," Molly said.

"But what?"

"I'm afraid of heights," she said.

"You went up the elevator of a New York City skyscraper, no problem," Finn reminded her. "And you stood at the top of the Empire State Building."

"I know," Molly said. "I guess I'm afraid of *falling* from heights . . . and it's easier to fall off a swinging rope than off a steady building."

"I can help you with this," Carlos said. "We just did ropes in gym class. I'll tell you what to do. Grip the rope with both hands. Keep your hands close together, one on top of the other. At the bottom, pinch the rope between your feet."

"Okay," Molly said. She followed Carlos's instructions. The rope swung back and forth a little bit. "Whoa."

Carlos grabbed the rope to steady it. "Don't worry, I'm spotting you. You can do this," he said. "Now take your top hand and move it higher. Good job. Same with your bottom hand. Keep the rope between your feet, but loosely, and move your feet up, too."

Carlos kept holding the rope steady as Molly inched her way up. Slowly but surely, she got to the opening in the ceiling where her brother waited. Finn grabbed Molly's hands and pulled her the rest of the way through. She wrapped her arms around her knees and sat with her head down to catch her breath, while Carlos took his turn climbing up the rope.

"Congratulations, you made it," Finn said when Carlos got to the top. "Along with a whole lot of fake Carloses—and fake Mollys, too."

"Huh?" Molly said. She looked around for the first time.

They weren't alone.

Hundreds of Carloses and Mollys and Finns were staring back at her.

"What . . . ? How . . . ?" she started.

"I believe the words you're looking for are 'holy guacamole,'" Finn said.

"That's right," she said. "Where are we?"

"I don't know," Finn said.

"Oh, I know!" Carlos said. "We must be in the Amazing Mirror Maze. I've always wanted to come here! It's across the street from the

Alamo. We must have gone underground to the other side of the River Walk."

"Was that rope here, just waiting for you?" Molly asked.

"Yep," Finn said. "Isn't that lucky?" He pulled the rope through the hole and put the trapdoor back in place.

"We must be on the right track," Carlos said.

"Or maybe someone was already here, and we're too late," Molly said.

"Even if someone else was here," Finn said, "*we* are the ones with the map."

"That's right," Carlos said. "Maybe the treasure is at the end of this mirror maze."

"Hmm . . . ," Molly said. "Can I see the map again?"

Carlos took the map out of his back pocket and handed it over.

Molly studied the map. "Look at this writing in the lower corner. It must be some kind of code."

"Maybe it's another secret language, like Roman numerals," Finn suggested.

$5 OFF QUESO DIP AT
THE RIVER WALK DINER

"I've never seen anything like this before," Molly said. "I'm stumped."

"I hate when you're stumped," Finn said.

"I'm over here," she said. A hundred different Mollys waved their hands.

Finn and Carlos both raised their hands, and a hundred different Finns and Carloses waved back.

Molly looked down to the map and walked around in circles, studying it. "Oh! I found a pathway out of this room," she said. "Follow me."

"Wait!" Carlos said. "How do we know which Molly to follow?"

"That's easy," Finn said. "We'll follow the one that disappears."

But when Molly ducked out of the room, *all* the Mollys disappeared.

"Oh, duh," Finn said. "If Molly herself disappears, of course all the reflections of Molly do, too. We have to go find her."

"Not just her," Carlos said. "We have to find my grandpa's map! She took it with her! I knew I shouldn't have trusted you guys. She probably wants to steal all the treasure for herself!"

"No way," Finn said. "My sister would never steal anything."

"She stole the map," Carlos said. "The only reason to steal the map is if she's planning to steal the treasure, too."

"You *gave* her the map," Finn said.

A hundred angry Carloses stared back at Finn. "You two no-accounts," the Carloses said. "I shouldn't have trusted you any farther than I can throw you."

"You're not big enough to throw us at all," Finn said.

"Exactly."

"Look, there's a pathway," Finn said. "Maybe it's the one Molly took. Let's go."

"Hang on," Carlos said. He picked up the rope. "We better hold on to this to make sure we're following each other and not our reflections. Here."

He held the end of the rope up toward Finn.

"That's not me," Finn said. "That's just my reflection."

Carlos handed the rope to another Finn, and another, and another. Finally, on the fifth try, he got the real Finn.

"Don't let go," Carlos said sternly.

"I won't," Finn said.

Carlos led them through mirrored turns, to a dark hallway with neon lights on the floor.

"Oh, it's so cool in here," Finn said.

"We can't stop," Carlos said. "Not until we find your sister."

They turned through an archway, into a circular, mirrored room. On the other side was a long hall filled with fun-house mirrors that stretched them into ten-foot-tall giants. "If I was this tall in real life, you wouldn't have needed to boost me out of the passageway," Finn said. "I'd have been able to move the trapdoor just by reaching up."

But then they turned a corner, and the next row of mirrors made them look like miniature people. "I'm even smaller than my baby brother," Carlos said.

He reached out to touch his reflection, and the mirror swung open, revealing one last mirrored room leading to the exit. And at the far side of that room was Molly!

"Finally! I've been waiting for you guys," she said.

"See, I told you she wasn't stealing the treasure," Finn told Carlos.

"You were right," Carlos said. "I'm sorry."

"It's okay."

"Come look at this," Molly said. She was holding the map up to the large mirrored wall. "I think I just cracked the code. And you're never going to believe it."

"You know where the treasure is?" Carlos asked.

"Not exactly." Molly nodded toward the mirror.

The writing was in English, but the words were backward and could only be read when held in front of a mirror.

$5 OFF QUESO DIP AT
THE RIVER WALK DINER

Chapter 10

THE RIVER WALK DINER

Molly, Finn, and Carlos walked back out into the blazing Texas sunshine. "A coupon?" Finn asked.

"Yep," Molly said.

"I know what dip is," Finn said. "But what's queso?"

"It's Spanish for 'cheese,'" Carlos said.

"Oh, yum!"

"But that can't be right," Carlos said.

"This map is over a hundred years old. Just look at it."

"Maybe it's a very old diner," Finn said. "Anyway, I'm starving."

"We might as well go check it out," Molly said.

She handed the map back to Carlos.

"Do you know where we are now?" Finn asked Molly.

"*I* know where we are," Carlos said. "This is the River Walk. It's probably the most famous spot in San Antonio—except for the Alamo, of course. That's the San Antonio River, and up above there is downtown."

"You mean we're walking *below* the town right now?" Molly asked.

"Uh-huh."

"Cool."

The River Walk was packed with families enjoying the summer day. Yellow fairy lights and cafe tables with brightly colored umbrellas lined the river.

Carlos led the way over an arched stone footbridge. Beneath them, a boat of tourists, snapping photos on their phones, passed by.

"Is it always this crowded?" Finn asked.

"Always," Carlos said.

"I love it here," Molly said.

"Apparently a lot of other people do, too," Finn said.

They came to a green-and-white-striped awning marking the River Walk Diner.

Carlos crossed his fingers. "Oh, Grandpa," he whispered. "I hope we're in the right place."

"Ready to go in?" Molly asked.

Carlos nodded, and they stepped inside. The diner had a black-and-white-tiled floor and red booths. A country song played on the jukebox.

"Table for three, please," Finn said.

The hostess led them to the last empty booth, near the kitchen, and handed them three menus. "Your waiter will be right with you," she said.

"We already know they serve cheese dip here," Finn said. "I mean *queso* dip. Good thing, because I'm starving."

"I just realized something," Molly said. "We can't order queso dip or anything else. We don't have any money."

"But we have a coupon," Finn said.

"The coupon means the queso dip costs less," said Molly. "It's not free." She picked up a menu. "The queso dip is seven dollars. But with five dollars off, it's two dollars."

"Oh," said Finn.

"I have money," Carlos said.

"I'll pay you back," Finn offered.

"That's okay," Carlos said. "Even if we don't find the treasure, I still think my grandpa would want me to share. And you can have all the dip. I'm not hungry anyway."

"You sound upset," Molly said.

"I am," Carlos said. "I thought we were on the right track . . . but this place is just a regular diner. So how could my great-great-great-great-great-grandfather's old treasure map have led us here?"

Finn shrugged.

"I don't know," Molly admitted.

Finn sighed and put his menu facedown on the table.

Molly glanced over. "What in the world . . . ?" she said.

"What's wrong?" Finn asked.

"The back of your menu," she said.

Carlos looked up, and then he quickly flipped over his own menu, too. "It's . . . it's . . ."

"Your great-great-great-great-great-grand-father's map," Molly supplied.

The menu version of the map was laminated in plastic. But when he spread both pieces of his map on the table next to the menu to compare them, there was no denying it. The maps were identical.

"But how . . . ," he started to ask.

A waiter arrived and placed three glasses of water on the table. "Hi there, I'm Tom, and I'll be your server today," he said. "What can I do for you?"

"You can tell us where these menus came from," Carlos said.

"Uh . . . ," Tom said. "The hostess brought them to you?"

"No, I mean, where did *this* come from?" Carlos asked. He tapped the picture of the treasure map.

"Oh, I don't know," Tom said. "You'll have to ask Sal about that."

"Who's Sal?" Molly asked.

"He owns this diner," Tom explained. "He's in charge of all menu decisions, and I'm in charge of orders. So what can I get you?"

"We'd like some queso dip," Finn said.

"And we'd like to talk to Sal," Carlos added.

"Dip coming right up," Tom said. "And I'll pass along the message to Sal."

Tom walked away, and Carlos bent his head toward Molly and Finn. "You know what I'm thinking," he said in a whisper.

"What?" the twins asked.

"I think Sal somehow got a copy of the map and found the buried treasure himself," Carlos said. "Then he used the money to buy this diner."

"But if the money was buried by your great-grandfather times five, then it really belongs to you," Molly said.

"Which means this is *your* diner," Finn said. "Holy guacamole. You're probably the youngest diner owner in the entire United States of America, and maybe even the world!"

"*Shh,*" Carlos said.

"Hello there," a voice boomed. The kids turned to see a man with twinkling brown eyes and a big handlebar mustache standing beside their table.

"Are you Sal?" Molly asked.

"Sure am," the man said. "Y'all have a question about the menu?"

"We have a question about the *back* of the menu," Carlos said. "This is an old map my grandpa gave me." He pushed the map across the table toward Sal. Then he placed the menu map beside it. "And this is the map on the back of your menu. They're the same!"

"Well, whaddya know," Sal said. "They are." He fingered Carlos's old map.

"Careful," Carlos said.

"Where'd you get this?" Sal asked.

"We should be asking you the same thing," Molly said. "Where'd *you* get the map that you have on the backs of all the menus?"

"An old friend gave it to me," Sal said.

"An old friend, huh?" Finn said. "The kind of old friend who dug up someone else's buried treasure?"

"Oh no, nothing like that," Sal said. He turned to Carlos. "Are you going to tell me where you got yours?"

"My grandpa Berto gave it to me," Carlos said.

"Ah," Sal said. "You must be Carlos."

Chapter 11

OLD FRIENDS

"It's a pleasure to finally meet you," Sal said.

"Finally meet me . . . ? You mean, you know who I am?" Carlos asked.

"I sure do," Sal said. "Your grandpa Berto and I were friends. He came here every week for strong coffee and some queso dip. Don't tell your grandma Rosa about the queso." Sal winked.

"You know my grandma, too?"

"No, I never met her," Sal said. "But I heard a lot about her. Berto talked about your whole family."

"Really?" Carlos asked.

"Sure thing," Sal said.

"He left the map in an envelope with my name on it," Carlos said. "But I don't understand. . . . Why would he give it to me if it's just a doodle from a diner menu?"

"It's not just any doodle," Sal said. "Your grandpa made that map himself."

"His *grandpa*?" Finn said. "But don't you mean his great-great-great-great-great-grandfather?"

"My great-grandfather times five fought in the Texas Revolution," Carlos explained. "When I saw the map, I thought that he must've buried treasure back then, and that Grandpa Berto wanted me to find it."

"Oh, no," Sal said. "Berto drew it, for sure. I was sitting right next to him when he did. You see, he was one of my first customers when I opened up shop. Back then, we didn't get much of a crowd. Berto thought the map would help lead tourists from the Alamo to the diner for a meal. We didn't ever get to distribute it at the Alamo. Turns out they didn't want their visitors digging things up in search of treasure over there. But I liked the drawing so much, I put it on the back of the menu. Berto said we should stain it with tea to make it look really old. Clever, huh?"

"Yeah," Carlos said.

"Anyway, it didn't matter," Sal said. "Business here at the diner picked up."

"There are still things that don't make sense," Molly said. "Carlos's grandpa only gave him half the map. The other half was behind a stone in the burial chamber. How'd that happen?"

"Well, I can't say for sure," Sal said. "But my guess is Carlos's grandpa was hoping to give Carlos a little adventure." He turned to Carlos. "You know what your grandpa always said...."

"No, what?" Carlos asked.

"He said, 'Money and riches are great to have, but true treasure is right here.'" Sal patted his chest. "What was in your grandpa's heart was what he treasured most. And that was you and your grandma. His family was the real treasure."

"So there's no gold?" Finn asked.

Sal laughed. "There's golden queso dip," he said. "Berto's favorite. Tom tells me you already ordered some. I reckon you'll enjoy it. It was nice to meet all of you—especially you, Carlos. You were your grandpa Berto's dearest treasure."

Carlos looked down at his hands. His eyes

got shiny again, and he blinked a bunch of times in a row.

"I'll go check on that queso now," Sal said. "Today it's on the house."

"Thanks," Carlos said.

"That's pretty cool that your grandpa left a big adventure for you," Finn said after Sal had left.

"Yeah . . . but are you mad that I don't have any gold or jewels to share with you?"

"Of course we're not mad," Finn said. "We got to meet you and go on a treasure hunt together. And we even get free queso dip."

"Oh!" Molly said. "I almost forgot!" She re-loosened the knot in her friendship bracelet and handed it to Carlos. "This is for you."

"Thanks." Carlos slipped the bracelet over his wrist and smiled.

Tom came back with the queso dip, along with tortilla chips and carrot sticks. The kids dug in.

"This is the best thing I've ever tasted," Finn said. "Your grandpa was on to something."

"Maybe we can make some when we get home," Molly said.

"Or you can come back to Texas and have some more with me," Carlos said.

"Oh yeah!"

They'd barely finished when a loud honk came from outside.

Finn's and Molly's eyes met across the table.

"I can't wait to tell Grandma Rosa all about this," Carlos said. "She loves stories about Grandpa Berto. I've missed him too much to talk to her about him. But talking about him with you made me feel a little bit better. Maybe if I tell Grandma this story, she'll feel better, too. Want to come over and tell her with me?"

The horn sounded again.

"Tell her we say hi and we hope to meet her next time we come to Texas," Molly said. "But right now we have to go. I'm sorry." She and Finn stood and hugged Carlos goodbye. Then they rushed out to meet PET.

Chapter 12

THE LONG WAY HOME

The camper was idling in the parking lot. Molly and Finn flew out of the diner and jumped inside.

"Buckle up, kids," PET said. "We're taking the long way home!"

Molly and Finn slid into their seats and clicked the seat belts shut.

"The long way?" Finn asked.

"Hold on!" said PET. The camper shook

from side to side. There was a flash of bright white light, and they took off. They flew past deserts and snaking rivers. Then they saw buildings and cars.

"Finn, take a look out of your window," PET said.

Finn did as he was told and saw a green field and a brown dirt diamond with ant-sized dots moving around it. "Is that Minute Maid Park?" he asked.

"That it is," PET said.

"Those ants must be the Houston Astros and the Cincinnati Reds!" Finn cried. "Good thing it's a clear night, so the stadium roof is wide open."

"Hey, PET," Molly said. "Why did you take us to San Antonio and not Houston? Is it because the teams didn't need any help,

but Carlos did? I mean, that's our work, right? Helping people?"

"That's right," PET said. "My instructions are to take you where help will be needed. The thing is, wherever you go, help is always needed."

"Your instructions?" Molly asked. "Who gave you instructions?"

PET didn't reply.

"Maybe you'll answer *this* question," Finn said. "I was really tired last night when we left Ohio. I didn't get to sleep at all, and we spent all day in Texas. So how come I'm not tired anymore?"

"You spent the day helping people, and that makes you feel good," PET said. "It's part of the magic."

"It was great to help Carlos," Molly

108

agreed. "But he's just one person—not *people*."

"But you did help *people*," PET said. "Think about it—you helped Carlos talk about his grandpa again, and that changed his life. Now he'll go home and tell his grandma a new story about his grandpa, and that will change hers. Who knows who else Carlos will help in the future, and his grandma, too. Imagine all the lives that could be changed just by helping one person in need."

"Wow," Finn said. "Who taught you all this stuff?"

Just then, the camper landed with a thud. PET's screen went dark, and the camper doors flung open.

"Huh . . . I guess PET isn't going to answer that question, either," Molly said. "Let's go home and have breakfast."

"You're forgetting something," Finn said.

He walked to the map at the back of the camper, picked up a blue pushpin, and stuck it into San Antonio, Texas.

"*Now* we can eat breakfast," he said. He followed Molly out of the camper and into the summer sunshine. It was good to be back in Ohio.

AUTHORS' NOTE

Thank you for reading about the Parker twins' latest adventure! This story is made up, but the Alamo is a real place in San Antonio. It's the site of an important battle in the Texas Revolution— the Battle of the Alamo.

The Battle of the Alamo took place over thirteen days, from February 23 to March 6, 1836. Texas colonists were fighting for independence from the Mexican government. The Mexican troops were led by General Santa Anna, and they far outnumbered the colonists. All the men who fought the Mexicans died, including Davy Crockett. The colonists lost the battle, but Texas did win its independence from Mexico in the end. On December 29, 1845, Texas became the twenty-eighth state of the United States.

Rumor has it that there may be treasure

buried in the walls or under the floorboards of the Alamo. Perhaps the colonists were hiding money or jewels for their families to find later. These rumors are what inspired this story.

Nearly everything that Carlos, Molly, and Finn encounter are things you'd see if you visited the Alamo today—there is a temporary sacristy, aka the monk's burial chamber (without windows) and an arcade (without video games). If you look carefully, you really can find some stones shaped like the state of Texas. Some people believe that spirits and ghosts haunt the Alamo . . . maybe that's why Finn was so worried about them!

One thing Carlos, Molly, and Finn find in this story that is *not* at the Alamo is the mysterious staircase hidden in a tree trunk. And while the Amazing Mirror Maze itself really exists, there is no secret underground passageway to the Amazing Mirror Maze. That came out of our own imaginations.

It's fun to make up stories, but even more fun to learn the real history! If you want to read more about the Texas Revolution and the Alamo, we recommend these books:

What Was the Alamo? by Pam Pollack and Meg Belviso

Who Was Davy Crockett? by Gail Herman

We hope you enjoyed our story and that it inspires you to have your own adventures!

Happy travels,
Courtney & Bianca

Texas State Facts

- The Texas state tree is the pecan. The state flower is the bluebonnet. The state bird is the mockingbird.

- The Texas state flag looks like this:

- Texas is the second biggest state in the United States. (The biggest state is Alaska.)

- Austin is the capital of Texas, and it is considered the live music capital of the whole world.

- Palo Duro canyon, also known as the Grand Canyon of Texas, is the second largest canyon in the United States. It lies in the Texas Panhandle, near the cities of Amarillo and Canyon. It is about 120 miles long, an average of 6 miles wide, and in some places, as much as 1,000 feet deep!

○ Texas is home to more species of bats than any other state. It has the largest-known bat colony in the whole world, Bracken Cave Preserve, which is located near San Antonio.

○ The official state mammal is not the bat; it's the armadillo. The name means "little armored one," because of their leathery armored shells.

○ Texas is also known as the Lone Star State, as a reminder of its struggle for independence from Mexico.

○ Millions of people visit the Alamo every year, where they can see artifacts from the battle, including a lock of the real Davy Crockett's hair, which is preserved in a glass locket at the Long Barrack Museum.

PET's favorite Texas fact:

○ The Texas state motto is "friendship."

N
W———E
S

AMARILLO ●

NM

TEX

EL PASO ●

● ODESSA

MEXICO ●

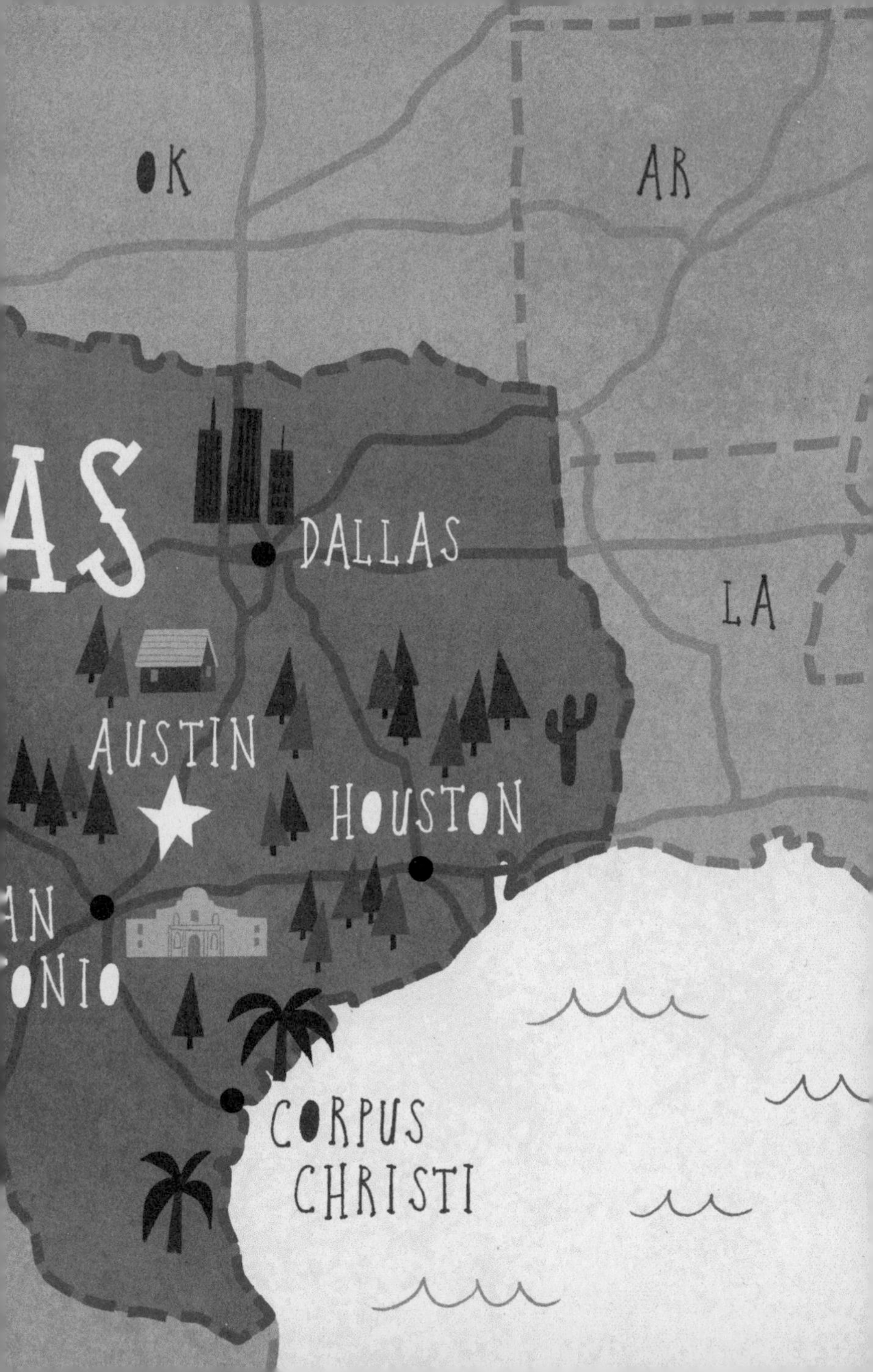
OK
AR
AS
DALLAS
LA
AUSTIN
HOUSTON
AN
ONIO
CORPUS
CHRISTI

Where will Finn and Molly go next?

Find out in
Escape from Camp California

Coming soon!

✪

Travel with Finn and Molly in the

MAGIC ON THE MAP books!

Have you read
them all?